For Grandma Thora,

with love and rich memories

of all your bedtime stories

Stories adapted by Stephen Krensky

Published in the United States by Random House, Inc., New York, and simultaneously in Canada

by Random House of Canada Limited, Toronto. Distributed by Random House, Inc., New York.

www.randomhouse.com/kids

Library of Congress Cataloging-in-Publication Data

Brown, Marc Tolon.

Arthur's really helpful bedtime stories / Marc Brown.

p. cm.

Summary: Ten classic tales, including "The Emperor's New Clothes," "Puss in Boots," and "The Frog Prince,"

are retold with Arthur the aardvark and his friends as characters in the stories.

ISBN 0-679-88468-8 (trade). – ISBN 0-679-98468-2 (lib. bdg.)

1. Fairy tales. [1. Fairy tales. 2. Folklore.] I. Title.

PZ8.B77Ar 1998 398.2–dc21

[E] 98-3663

Printed in the United States of America

10 9 8 7 6 5 4 3 2 1

Arthur's Really Helpful BEDTIME STORIES

Marc Brown

Random House 🏠 New York

CONTENTS

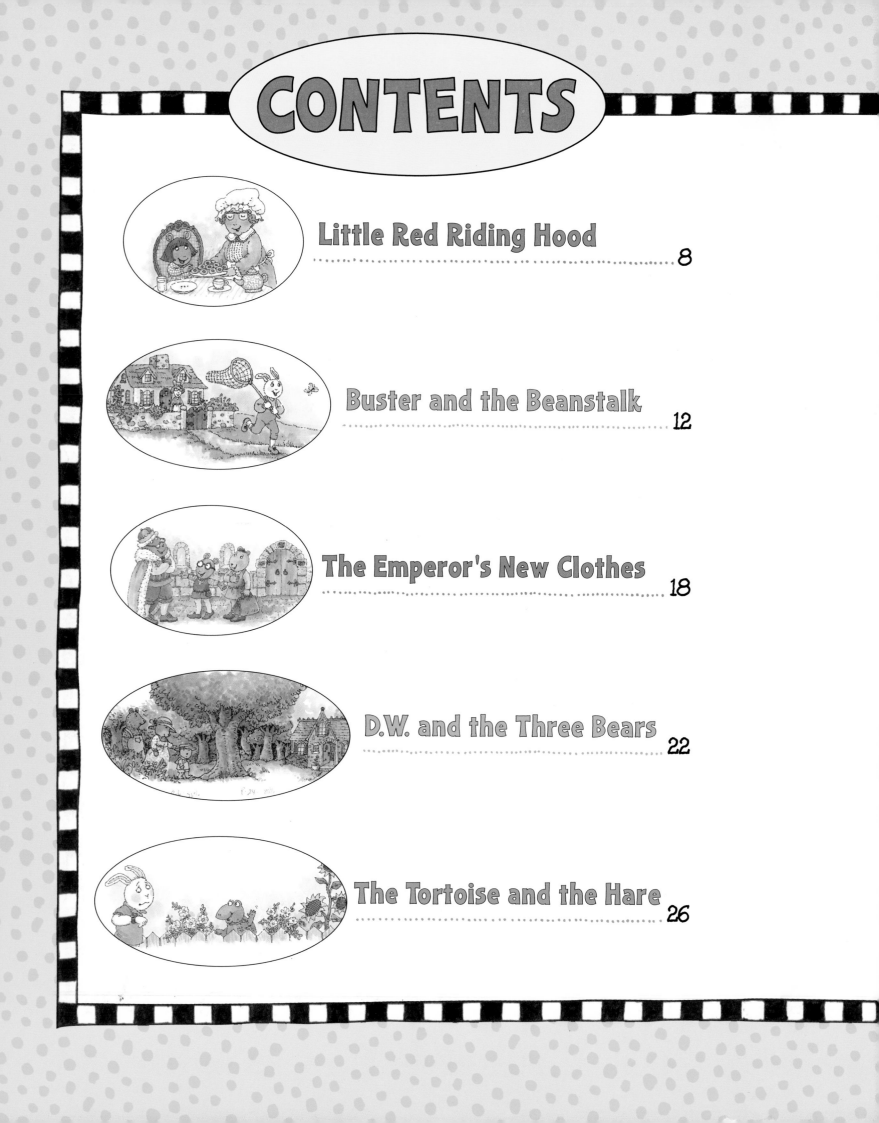

Little Red Riding Hood

There once was a little girl whose favorite color was red. She liked red skirts, red shoes, and even red underwear. Most of all, she liked her red cape with a hood, which she wore every chance she got.

"Aren't you tired of red yet?" her mother asked each morning.

"No," said D.W., for that was the little girl's name. "Once I decide I like something, I like it forever."

One day, her father, a very good cook, made some food for D.W. to take to her grandmother.

"Grandma Thora always enjoys my home-baked bread," he said. "And I've made some raspberry jam, too."

So D.W. set off for her grandmother's house, which was over the river and through the woods.

Along the way, she met a wolf.

"Good morning," said the wolf.

"Hello," said D.W.

The wolf licked his lips. "Where are you going on such a fine day?" he asked.

"To my grandmother's house," said D.W. "And could you please be more careful? You're drooling on my cape."

Now, the wolf was very hungry. He wanted to eat D.W. up, cape and all, right then and there. But he decided to be a little more patient and perhaps be rewarded with two delicious meals instead of just one.

"And where does your grandmother live?" he asked.

"In a very neat house over the river and through the woods," said D.W. "I always have to wipe my feet before I go inside."

Hmmm?

"I'll keep that in mind," said the wolf, darting off into the deep dark woods.

When D.W. got to Grandma Thora's house, she saw big muddy paw prints on the doormat. "Hmmm, that's funny," she said to herself as she wiped both her feet before going inside.

"Hello, Grandma Thora!" she called out. "It's me, D.W. Where are you?"

"In here, my dear," said a strange deep voice from the bedroom.

D.W. stepped into the kitchen for a moment, then skipped into the bedroom. There she saw a figure in her grandmother's bed. The figure was wearing Grandma Thora's nightgown and cap.

"I have brought you some good things to eat," said D.W.

"So you have," said the figure.

D.W. came closer. "Oh, Grandma Thora!" she said. "I never noticed before what big ears you have."

"The better to hear you with, my dear."

D.W. looked again. "Oh, Grandma Thora!" she said. "And what big eyes you have!"

"The better to see you with, my dear."

D.W. came right up next to the bed.

"Oh, Grandma Thora!" she said. "What big teeth you have—and I'm not sure you've been brushing regularly."

"The better to eat you with, my dear!" cried the wolf, throwing back the blanket.

But the wolf was not used to wearing a nightgown. As he leapt out of bed, the nightgown caught on the bedpost. The wolf tripped and fell hard to the floor. CRASH! Then D.W. pulled out a big iron frying pan. She had picked it up in Grandma's kitchen and hidden it in her hood. BONK! She knocked the wolf out with it.

"Thank you for remembering to wipe your feet," she said to the wolf, even though he couldn't hear her.

"D.W., is that you?" came a muffled voice from the closet.

"Yes, it is," said D.W. She unlocked the closet door and there she found her grandmother, safe and sound, and very happy to see D.W.

"Oh, my!" said Grandma Thora, looking around. "I see you've been busy. Thank goodness the wolf didn't have time to eat me before you arrived. Why don't we go fetch the hunter who lives next door? He'll take care of the wolf for us."

Once the hunter had come and gone, D.W. and her grandmother sat down for lunch.

"You look really good in red," said Grandma Thora.

"Thank you," said D.W. "My red riding hood came in *very* handy today."

And she wore her red riding hood for many days after that.

Buster and the Beanstalk

In an old cottage outside of town lived a poor boy named Buster and his mother. Buster always meant to do what his mother told him, but sometimes he forgot. It was hard to milk the cow on a perfect day for fishing. And it was hard to rake up the hay when jumping in it was so much more fun.

Things for the family went from bad to worse, until one day Buster's mother told him they must sell the cow.

"She's starting to give less milk," his mother explained. "We need to sell her while she's still worth something."

So the next morning, Buster and the cow started on their way to market. It was a sunny day, just right for chasing butterflies, and Buster was sorry he had a job to do.

"Good morning, Buster!" said an old man by the side of the road.

Buster was surprised. "How do you know my name?" he asked.

"Oh, you just look like a Buster. Smart. Dignified."

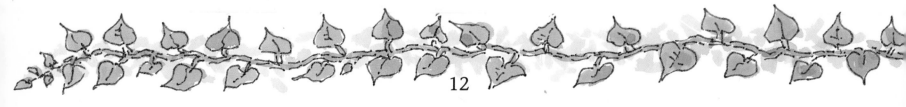

Buster was pleased.

"And where are you going?" the man asked.

"To market," said Buster. "I have to sell our cow."

"What a pity having to go all that way on such a fine day for chasing butterflies."

Buster nodded.

"What if I saved you the trouble?" said the old man. "Will you trade your cow for these five beans?" He held out his hand.

Buster just laughed. "I wouldn't trade our cow for some silly beans. I'm smart, remember?"

"Ah, but these beans are very special. They're magic beans."

Buster thought it over. Magic beans were surely worth a lot. And the butterflies were just waiting to be chased.

When Buster got home, his mother was surprised to see him.

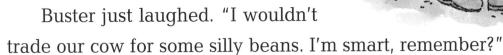

"Back so soon?" she said. "You must have gotten a good price."

Buster held out his hand. "Even better," he said. "I got these five magic beans!"

"Beans? You sold our cow for magic beans?" his mother shouted. "We need money, not beans."

She angrily threw them out the window and sent Buster to his room.

The next morning, when Buster woke up, he looked outside and saw a beanstalk growing toward the sky.

"I wonder where it goes," said Buster.

He went out and started climbing. By the time he got to the top, the beanstalk had poked through the clouds. Buster looked around. He could see a castle in the distance. As he got closer, he could see it was a giant's castle. When he arrived there, Buster found that he couldn't reach the doorknob. But he was able to slide under the door.

"Hello!" Buster called out. "Anybody home?"

No one answered. Suddenly, though, the room began to shake. Buster nervously hid behind a broom in the corner.

The shaking got louder and louder. Then the door burst open— and a giant came in. CLOMP! CLOMP! CLOMP! he stomped as he glanced around quickly, sniffing the air.

"Fee, fi, fo, fum!
As I was coming up the path,
I smelled someone who needs a bath."

Buster bit his lip. He had been meaning to wash up, but he just hadn't gotten around to it.

The giant might have found him if he had searched, but he was distracted by a fluttering noise. He went over to a small birdcage and peered at the goose inside.

Buster was surprised. "Why would the giant keep an ordinary goose around?" Buster wondered. "It would barely make a snack for him. He must be an awfully mean giant to keep the poor bird all cooped up in a small cage."

The giant lifted the cage to a table. "Lay!" he ordered the goose.

The next moment, the goose laid an egg. Buster could see immediately that it was no ordinary egg. This egg was made of solid gold!

The giant admired it greedily for a moment. Then he yawned mightily and laid his head on the table to take a short nap.

His snoring soon filled the room like thunder.

Buster took a deep breath. "Now's your chance," he thought.

"Your chance to be squashed like a bug," his thoughts replied.

"Well, I can't just stay here forever. And as long as I'm leaving, I might as well make the most of it."

There was no answer to that, and so Buster climbed up the table, opened the cage, and took out the goose.

The goose started honking and flapping its wings.

"Quiet!" Buster whispered. "I'm trying to rescue you."

Luckily, the giant couldn't hear anything over the sound of his own snoring.

The goose went right on honking, but Buster held her tightly and ran for his life. Just as he reached the beanstalk, he heard a roar from the castle.

"WHO STOLE MY GOOSE?!"

Buster started climbing down the beanstalk in a hurry. Considering the giant's keen sense of smell, Buster knew he didn't have much of a head start.

When he reached the ground, he shouted to his astonished mother, "Hold this goose and move back!"

Then he ran to get his ax.

The beanstalk was already shaking a little from the weight of the giant high above. As fast as he could, Buster swung the ax.

CHOP! CHOP! CHOP!

With the last cut, Buster jumped back. The whole beanstalk came crashing down—and the giant with it.

When the dust cleared, there was a huge pit in the ground.

"Well," said Buster, dusting off his hands. "I guess I wasn't the one squashed like a bug, after all."

With golden eggs to sell, Buster and his mother were able to build a big new house and start living in style. Best of all, there was plenty of time for Buster to chase all the butterflies he could find.

The Emperor's New Clothes

Long ago, there was an emperor who loved to wear beautiful clothes. He wore a different outfit to every meal and rarely wore the same thing twice.

One day, two visitors came to the emperor's palace. They told everyone they were weavers.

"We weave the best cloth," said one, called the Brain. "Pure fiber, organically grown."

"Our cloth is so fine," said the other, whose name was Arthur, "that it is invisible to foolish people."

When the emperor heard this, he invited the two weavers to make him some clothes.

The weavers agreed. "We will need a nice place to work," said Arthur. "No distractions like pesky little sisters. And plenty of snacks."

"We must also have gold thread and the finest silk," the Brain added. "Our designs depend on it."

"Yes, yes," said the emperor, "whatever you want."

He gave the weavers a large room with a view of the garden. Every day, whenever anyone came by, they sat before their loom, pretending to weave. The rest of the time they ate and slept and played games. As for the silk and gold thread, they hid them under the bed.

After a week, the curious emperor sent his prime minister to see them.

"Our work is going very well," the weavers told her. "Come in and see for yourself." They pointed to the loom.

The prime minister opened her eyes wide. She rubbed them twice. It didn't help. She still saw no cloth. "Does this mean I am foolish?" she thought to herself. "How terrible! Nobody must find out."

"Do you like the colors?" asked Arthur.

"Dramatic, aren't they?" said the Brain.

The prime minister sighed. "I've never seen anything like them," she admitted, and told the emperor the same thing.

When another week had passed, the curious emperor sent the lord chamberlain for a peek.

"Come in," the weavers told him. "Take a good look."

The lord chamberlain stared and stared. Like the prime minister, he couldn't see a thing.

"Am I so foolish?" he thought. "Oh, dear. No one must find out."

"So what do you think?" asked Arthur. "Pretty amazing, huh?"

"Oh, my," said the lord chamberlain. "It's hard to put into words. But I'm certainly glad everything is going so well."

And that's what he told the emperor.

After a third week had passed, the emperor himself came to see the cloth. He was escorted by both the prime minister and the lord chamberlain.

"You've arrived at a crucial moment," said the Brain. "As you will see, this part is rather tricky."

As their guests watched, the weavers continued with their work. First they pretended to take the cloth off the loom. Then they pretended to cut it into pieces. Finally, they pretended to sew the pieces together.

The emperor coughed to hide his confusion. He could see no cloth at all.

"Is anything wrong, Your Majesty?" asked the Brain.

"No, no," said the emperor. "Your work simply took my breath away. I couldn't be happier." He paused. "There's to be a parade tomorrow. Will the clothes be ready by then?"

"We will do our best," Arthur said. "Keep those snacks coming."

The next morning, the emperor arrived to get dressed. The weavers lifted their arms as though clothing were draped over them.

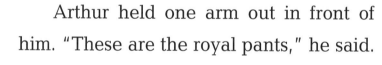

Arthur held one arm out in front of him. "These are the royal pants," he said.

The Brain held out both arms. "And this is the royal robe."

"Ah," said the emperor.

"The clothing is very light," the Brain went on. "You will almost feel as though you are wearing nothing at all."

The weavers pretended to lift each piece of clothing and place it on the emperor. When they were done, they stood back and clapped their hands.

"What style!" cried Arthur.

"What grace!" agreed the Brain.

"What . . . a surprise," said the emperor. He looked hard in the mirror—and sighed.

The emperor led the parade up and down the city streets. In all the commotion, nobody noticed the two weavers leaving by the back gate with a sack filled with royal snacks.

Everyone knew the story of the emperor's new clothes and how only foolish people couldn't see them. So they all spoke up quickly: "Did you ever see such a robe?" "What colors!" "The emperor never looked better."

One little girl, though, was not so impressed. She looked at the emperor and laughed. "But he doesn't have anything on!" she cried.

As if a spell had been broken, the crowd began to laugh, too: "She's right, isn't she?" "He isn't wearing a thing." "He has nothing on at all!"

The emperor bit his lip—and blushed right down to his toes. He knew they were right, but he wasn't going to admit it.

He kept his head high as the laughter followed him all the way through the town and back to the palace.

D.W. and the Three Bears

There was once a little girl named D.W. who often did the opposite of what she was told.

When her mother explained that she had to be gentle with some toys, she played roughly with them until they broke.

If her father said that a fresh batch of cookies was too hot to eat, she always took a bite, anyway.

And when her big brother warned her about reading scary stories at bedtime, D.W. read the scariest stories she could find, even though they gave her bad dreams.

One day, D.W. went out for a walk in the woods. Her mother told her not to go far, so naturally D.W. wandered farther than she had ever gone before.

She came upon a little cottage where the door was open. A delicious smell was coming from inside. Now, D.W. had been told many times not to go into strange houses—so, of course, that was the first thing she did.

Inside, she found three bowls of oatmeal cooling on the table. She took a taste from the biggest bowl, but it was too hot. She took a taste from the medium-size bowl, but it was too cold. Then she took a taste from the smallest bowl.

"Just right," she decided, and quickly gobbled it up.

Then she went into the living room. There she saw three chairs. The biggest chair was too hard for her. The medium-size chair was too soft. The smallest one, though, looked just right. But when D.W. sat down on it, the chair broke in pieces.

"They sure don't make things like they used to," said D.W., as she picked herself up off the floor.

Upstairs, D.W. found three beds in a row. She bounced on the first bed. "Too hard," she thought. She bounced on the second. It was softer, but not quite right.

The third bed, though, was perfect. In fact, she bounced on it so long that she got very tired. Snuggling under the blanket, D.W. fell fast asleep.

While D.W. was sleeping, the family of three bears returned to their cottage. They noticed at once that all was not well.

"Someone's been eating my oatmeal," said the big Papa Bear.

"Someone's been eating my oatmeal, too," said the middle-sized Mama Bear.

"Someone's been eating my oatmeal!" said the little Baby Bear. "And they've eaten it all up."

The three bears then went into their living room.

"I think someone's been sitting in my big chair," said Papa Bear.

"Someone's been sitting in my chair, too," said Mama Bear.

"And someone's been sitting in my little chair," said Baby Bear. "And now it's broken all apart."

The bears were not happy about this. They marched upstairs to see what else might be wrong.

CLOMP! CLOMP! CLOMP!

"Someone's been sleeping in my bed!" roared Papa Bear.

"Someone's been sleeping in my bed, too!" growled Mama Bear.

"Someone's been sleeping in my bed!" gasped Baby Bear. "And she's still there! Look at her!"

The three angry bears stood by Baby Bear's bed.

They glared down at D.W.

Just then, she opened her eyes.

"Oh, my!" she cried. "I'm in big trouble."

She leapt up, bouncing past the bears from one bed to the next. Then she ran down the stairs and out the front door.

The three bears never saw the girl again—and they didn't miss her one bit. As for D.W. herself, she got home safely before dark. The very next day, she began doing what she was told—except that she refused to ever eat oatmeal again.

The Tortoise and the Hare

There was once a tortoise and a hare who lived near each other, but didn't speak very often. The reason they didn't speak was that the hare was always in a hurry.

"Hello, hello," the hare would say if they happened to meet on the road. "Buster's my name and running's my game."

"Good morning," said the tortoise.

"Can't talk now," Buster would say. "I've got places to go and things to do." And to prove his point, he would then disappear in a flash.

At one such meeting, though, the tortoise finally put in a few words.

"You really should slow down," he declared. "All this rushing around isn't good for you. Can you name any of the flowers you see on this road every day? Have you ever stopped to smell them? No. You're in too much of a hurry."

Buster took a moment to laugh in the tortoise's face—and then he was off again, even faster than before.

The next time their paths crossed, the tortoise added something else.

"Faster is not *always* better," he said.

For the first time, Buster came to a screeching halt.

"What? What did you say?"

The tortoise repeated his words.

"Oh, really?" said Buster. "Well, talk is cheap. Let's have a race to prove it. If I win, I get to train you into a world-class runner."

"And if I win," said the tortoise, "we'll have a long, slow breakfast together every day, and I'll teach you all about the flowers."

"Done!" said Buster.

The race was set for the following day. "You can start us," Buster said, jogging in place.

The tortoise nodded. "Ready. Set. Go!"

Before the tortoise could even blink, Buster was already ten yards down the road. Still, the tortoise was not discouraged, and he ambled off at his own slow pace.

Soon Buster was so far ahead that he couldn't even see the tortoise.

"No point in hurrying," Buster said. Then he yawned. He had to admit that all this rushing about *was* a little tiring. "In fact," he decided, "I might as well sit down and take a rest."

He found a comfortable spot in the shade. It was so comfortable, in fact, that he fell fast asleep.

He was snoring loudly when the tortoise passed him, and he was still dreaming when the tortoise crossed the finish line.

"Unfair!" Buster protested when he finally awoke.

"I don't see why," said the tortoise.

Buster really didn't, either. And so he kept his word, meeting the tortoise every day for breakfast. Before a month was up, the two of them had become good friends. Just as important, Buster finally stopped to smell the flowers, and even though some of them made him sneeze, he was too polite to mention it.

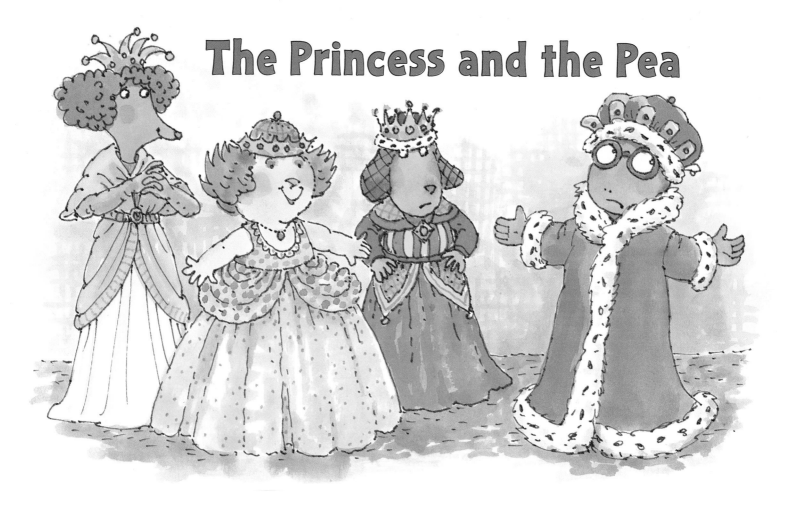

The Princess and the Pea

There was once a prince who was eager to fall in love. But being a prince, he had to fall in love with a princess.

So his parents introduced him to princesses from lands near and far. There were short princesses and tall ones, thin princesses and fat ones. There were even a few so overdressed it was hard to know what they really looked like at all.

One night, during a terrible storm, the prince was having dinner with his parents at their castle.

"I'm afraid we're running out of princesses," noted the king.

"We mustn't give up hope," the queen insisted.

The prince just sighed, pushing the food around on his plate.

After dinner, there was a loud pounding at the castle door, and a young woman was brought in. She was splashed with mud, and her dripping clothing made puddles on the floor.

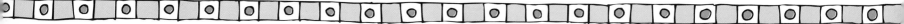

"Good evening, Your Majesties," she said, shaking rain from her hair. "I am Princess Francine. Thanks for letting me in."

The prince could hardly believe his eyes. He had never seen such a bedraggled princess before.

The king and queen were also surprised.

"What great need made you travel on such a night?" the king asked.

"Nothing special," the princess explained. "I've just recently arrived in your kingdom, and I thought I would go out for a ride."

"Even in a storm?" asked the queen.

Princess Francine shrugged. "A little rain doesn't bother me. But the thunder spooked my horse, and she threw me. I'll find her in the morning."

The prince didn't know what to think. Here was a brave and resourceful princess, unlike any he had met before.

The queen knew her son well and could see the look that had come over his face. But what did they really know of Francine? They had to find out if she was really a princess.

And for that, the queen had a plan.

"Come," she said to Francine.

"Let's get you into some dry clothing and find you a room."

While Francine was changing, the queen had twenty mattresses piled on a bed. Under the bottom one, she placed a single pea.

When Francine arrived in her bedroom, she was impressed.

"That's quite a bed," she said, looking up. "Luckily, I'm not afraid of heights." Ignoring the ladder, she scrambled up the mattresses and settled in.

"Sleep well," said the queen, closing the door behind her.

"If she's really a princess, we'll know soon enough," she said to herself.

The next morning, Francine met the royal family at breakfast.

"And how are you feeling this morning?" the queen asked.

Francine yawned. "I hardly slept at all. I kept feeling as if I was lying on a sharp rock. I even turned black and blue."

The queen smiled. Only a true princess could have felt the pea through twenty king-size mattresses.

The prince was delighted, too, and began spending as much time as possible with Francine. Soon they were both in love with each other.

After the prince and princess were married, they continued to sleep on the twenty mattresses because Francine liked the view. The prince removed the pea, though, so that they could sleep happily ever after.

The Three Little Pigs

Once upon a time, there were three little pigs who were arguing over how to build their clubhouse.

"Let's do it fast," said the first little pig. "If we use straw, we can be done in a few minutes. Then we can play."

"Not too fast," said the second little pig. "We have to take this seriously. Sticks would be stronger than straw."

"That's right," said the third little pig. "We should do it very carefully. Bricks are even stronger than sticks. We want a clubhouse that will last."

Well, the pigs kept arguing and arguing without getting anywhere. They were making so much noise that Arthur, Binky, and the Brain asked what was the matter, and the pigs explained.

"I agree with the first pig," said Binky.

"I agree with the second," said Arthur.

"I agree with the third," said the Brain. "You can never be too careful."

"In that case," said Arthur, "maybe we should build three clubhouses and stop arguing."

So that's what they did.

The first little pig and Binky finished first. "That's the last straw," said Binky, putting it into place and looking pleased.

They sat down to relax.

"This is the life," said the first little pig.

"I'll say," Binky agreed.

Just then, there was a knock at the door. The first little pig looked out.

"It's the wolf," he hissed.

"Is that bad?" asked Binky.

The pig nodded. "Go away!" he shouted.

The wolf didn't budge. "I want to join your club," he said.

"Don't believe him," the first little pig told Binky. "He's not just *any* wolf. He's the Big Bad Wolf. I'll bet he wants to eat me.

"Go away!" he told the wolf again.

But the wolf would not listen. "If you don't let me in, I'll huff and I'll puff and I'll blow your house down."

The first little pig still said no.

So the wolf HUFFED. . . and he PUFFED. . . and he BLEW the clubhouse of straw down.

Binky and the first little pig ran lickety-split to the second little pig's clubhouse.

"Let us in, Arthur!" yelled Binky. "The wolf is coming!"

Soon the wolf was knocking at the door of the clubhouse of sticks.

"I want to join your club," he said.

But the second little pig didn't believe the wolf, either.

"Go away!" he squealed.

But the wolf would not listen. "If you don't let me in, I'll huff and I'll puff and I'll blow your house down."

The second little pig still said no.

So the wolf HUFFED . . . and he PUFFED . . . and he BLEW the clubhouse of sticks down.

Binky, Arthur, and the two little pigs ran lickety-split down the hill to the third little pig's clubhouse.

The Brain and the third little pig were busily laying bricks.

"What's wrong?" they asked.

The two little pigs explained.

"I think we'll be safe here," said the Brain. "The reinforced concrete is earthquake-resistant."

"Let's not forget the steel I-beams," said the third little pig. "They're rated to withstand a Force 3 hurricane."

Arthur took a deep breath. "I only hope it's enough," he said.

They all helped to finish laying the bricks. They were just cleaning up when the wolf appeared at the door.

"I want to join your club," he growled, licking his lips. Blowing down the two other houses had given him quite an appetite.

"Go away!" squealed the third little pig.

But the wolf would not listen. "If you don't let me in, I'll huff and I'll puff and I'll blow your house down."

But the third little pig still said no.

So the wolf HUFFED . . . and he PUFFED . . . and he BLEW . . . and he BLEW . . . and he BLEW.

But the third house, the house made of bricks—with the reinforced-concrete foundation and the steel I-beams—withstood the blast.

When the wolf saw that he could not blow down the clubhouse of bricks, he slunk off into the woods.

The three little pigs cheered.

"I doubt we've seen the last of him," said the Brain. "There is still one way for him to get in." He looked at the chimney.

"But we can solve that problem," said the third little pig, who began laying logs in the fireplace. Then he started a cozy fire.

As night fell, the wolf returned and snuck up on the roof.

"I'll surprise them all," he snarled, then jumped down the chimney—and landed in the blazing fire!

"YOWL!" cried the wolf.

Out the door ran the wolf, howling about his burned bottom—and he never came back to join their club again.

The Frog Prince

There was once a princess named Muffy who was very rich and very spoiled. Her bedroom took up a whole tower of a castle, and it was filled with toys. She had four closets to hold all her clothes—one for each season—and two servants whose only jobs were to buy whatever Muffy wanted.

But of all her possessions, the one she loved the most was a golden ball. It had been a gift from her parents, and it shone like the sun at noon.

One day, the princess was playing with her ball in the garden when it fell into the well—SPLASH!—and sank right to the bottom.

"Oh, no!" Muffy cried as she looked down the well.

"What is wrong, Princess?" asked a voice nearby.

She answered without even looking up. "I have lost my precious golden ball down the well."

"I will get the ball for you," said the voice.

"You will? How wonderful!"

The princess looked up—and found herself staring at a frog. It wasn't a bad-looking frog, as frogs go, but still it was rather slimy and yellowy green.

"I will bring you the ball," said the frog, "if you grant me but one wish."

"Yes, yes, anything," said the princess. "Flies served on a silver platter? A jewel-encrusted lily pad? What do you want?"

"I want you to be my friend."

The princess was surprised, but she was in no mood to argue. "Fine, fine. I can do that."

But the frog was not done yet. "Not just *any* friend. Best friends. I want us to eat together and play together, and even live in the same room."

"All right, all right," said the princess impatiently. This frog certainly was a talker. "I promise. Now get the ball."

"As you wish," he said, and dove into the well. A short time later, he returned, and held the gleaming ball out to the princess.

"Hooray!" she cried as she snatched it away and skipped down the path.

"Remember your promise," the frog called after her.

But Princess Muffy didn't answer.

That night, a servant interrupted the royal family during dinner.

"Sire," he informed the king, "there's a frog outside who says he's here to see the princess."

The king almost choked on a roll. "A frog? The princess?"

"Yes, sire. He says they're very good friends."

The king looked at his daughter.
"Is this true?" he asked.

Princess Muffy blushed.

"In a way . . ."

"In *what* way?" the king demanded.

Princess Muffy explained about the frog and her promise.

"You have given your word," said the king. "Now you must keep it."

Sighing deeply, Princess Muffy told the servant to let the frog in.

The frog quickly hopped over to the table and onto the chair next to Princess Muffy. "I hope I didn't miss much," he said.

The king cleared his throat. "We all appreciate what you did for the

princess. Would you like some dinner?"

"Thank you, I'll just share with Muffy. That's what friends do," said the frog, and he began investigating the food on her plate. "No fresh flies, I see, but I won't go hungry."

Princess Muffy suddenly lost her appetite, but she sat politely until the meal was over. Then she led the frog to her room.

"This is a very fine room," he said. "I especially like the bed." He hopped up on the blanket. "So nice and soft."

The princess wondered if she would ever get a good night's sleep there again. But she managed to smile weakly, remembering her promise.

"Will you be coming to bed soon?" the frog asked.

"Um, I think I'll sit up and read for a while," said the princess.

"As you wish. Good night, then," said the frog, getting comfortable under the covers.

When Princess Muffy woke the next morning, she was stiff from sleeping in her chair. For a moment, she wondered why she wasn't in bed. But then she remembered all about the frog.

She looked over to her bed, expecting to see the frog doing some kind of froggy thing on the pillow.

But the frog was gone, and a young prince was lying in his place. He was watching her.

"Who are you?" asked the astonished princess. "And where's the frog?"

The prince sat up. "My name's Arthur. I am the frog—or at least I was. A wicked witch turned me into a frog. She said the spell would hold until I found a princess who would be my friend." He smiled. "Because you kept your promise to me, the spell was broken. I can never thank you enough. But perhaps we can be even better friends from now on."

"Oh, yes!" Princess Muffy declared happily, and they went off to play together.

The Lion and the Mouse

A mouse was once running through the jungle when suddenly he was pounced on and captured.

"GRRrrr!" roared a voice above him.

The mouse wriggled and squirmed, but he could not break free.

"It is useless to struggle," said the voice. The voice belonged to Binky.

The mouse looked up in terror.

"Of course you are afraid," Binky went on. "You have been captured by the King of Beasts."

The mouse feared for his life, but he could not help exclaiming, "You? The King of Beasts? You don't look much like a lion."

"YOU ARE IN NO POSITION TO ARGUE!" Binky shouted at him. "I roar like a lion. I say I'm big like a lion. And," he added, baring his teeth, "I eat like a lion."

The mouse saw his point. "Are you g-going to eat me?" he asked.

Binky hesitated. "I'm considering it."

"You really shouldn't go to all that bother," said the mouse. "There isn't much to me, when you stop to think about it. I'd barely make a mouthful for you. Not even a good snack."

"You talk a lot for a mouse," said Binky. "But I suppose you're right. The King of Beasts can show mercy."

He released his grip and let the mouse go.

It was not much later that Binky found himself caught in a hunter's trap. No matter how he twisted and turned, the ropes held him tight.

Far away, the mouse heard a roar. "That sounds like the King of Beasts," he said. "He may be in trouble. Perhaps I'd better check."

The mouse scurried through the jungle until he came upon Binky trapped in the net.

"So, King of Beasts, we meet again," said the mouse in his small voice.

Binky was too tired to roar, but he managed a little snarl.

"Calm down," said the mouse. "I'm here to help. After all, one good turn deserves another. Now hold still."

And working very carefully, little by little, the mouse chewed through the ropes.

"Thank you," said Binky when he was free once more.

"You're welcome, Your Majesty," said the mouse. "I only hope that every lion I meet will be as kind as you."

"Don't count on it," said Binky. "I *am* pretty special."

41

Puss in Boots

There was once a young man named Arthur who owned nothing more than the ragged clothes on his back, and he had only his cat, Puss, for company. But Puss was no ordinary cat. For one thing, he could talk. And for another, he wore soft leather boots.

"Life is hard," sighed the young man. "But at least there's no pesky homework."

"Do not worry, Arthur," said Puss. "If you follow my advice, you will make your fortune."

Arthur knew the cat was clever, having seen him catch mice twelve different ways, but he couldn't imagine how Puss could make him rich.

For several weeks, Puss went out and caught rabbits and ducks every day. Some of his catch he shared with Arthur. The rest he took to the king. And with every gift, he always included a note: *With the compliments of the Duke of Lakewood.*

One day, when Puss learned that the king would be passing by the river, he told Arthur to go for a swim. "But leave your clothes hidden under this bush."

"Even my *underwear?*" asked Arthur.

The cat nodded. "Yes, even your underwear."

"This is so embarrassing," said Arthur. But he did as Puss told him, and enjoyed himself paddling about in the reeds. Soon the king's coach came down the road, just as the cat had told him it would. The king and his daughter were inside.

Puss ran out waving his paws. "Help! Help! My master, the Duke of Lakewood, is drowning!"

The king recognized the cat who was always bringing him gifts. He ordered the coach to stop and pointed his servants in Arthur's direction.

Now, Arthur was a good swimmer and in no danger at all, but following the cat's instructions, he allowed himself to be rescued.

"Uh-oh, I don't think the duke has any clothes," said the princess, whose eyesight was quite good.

"Oh, no!" cried Puss in Boots. "A band of thieves must have stolen them while the duke was swimming."

"How terrible," said the king. He immediately commanded his servants to give the duke something to wear.

In his new clothes, Arthur looked rather grand. He made a very good impression on the king's daughter.

"It is good to meet you at last," said the king. "Where is your home?"

"The duke has a fine castle not many miles from here," said Puss.

Arthur blinked. "I do?"

"It's sometimes hard for the duke to keep track of his homes," Puss went on. "He has so many. Perhaps after you have rested, you would like to continue on there for dinner."

"Excellent," said the king. "I'd like nothing better."

Arthur might have objected to this, but he didn't. The prospect of remaining with the princess a little longer made him very happy.

The cat now had his work cut out for him. He ran ahead down the road until he came to the grand castle he had told the king about. It was really the home of a feared ogre who had magical powers.

The cat knocked at the door, and the ogre let him in.

"O mighty one," said Puss, "I have come a great distance to meet you and stand in the shadow of your greatness."

The ogre smiled. He liked the way this cat talked.

"I have heard," Puss continued, "that you have the gift of being able to change into any animal you choose."

"See for yourself," said the ogre, and in an instant he became a huge and fierce lion.

"Goodness!" said Puss, who was somewhat relieved when the ogre returned to his original form.

"Such a sight was worth my journey in itself. But I wonder . . . oh, never mind."

"No, no, tell me," the ogre insisted.

"Well, I was wondering if you could also take the form of a small animal, one quite different from your actual size."

"Of course!" boasted the ogre, and promptly turned himself into a mouse.

"Very good," said Puss. Then he pounced on the mouse and ate him up.

By the time the king's coach arrived, Puss had a delicious feast waiting for them. It is said that the Duke of Lakewood and the princess were later married, but if so, Puss had nothing to do with it. Some things, he was heard to observe, have to happen on their own.